Emerson,

Believe in yourself
and you will go far.

JOE-JOE NUT AND BISCUIT BILL ADVENTURES

CASE # 2:

MINERAL MISCHIEF

RENÉE HAND

NORTH STAR PRESS OF ST. CLOUD, INC.
St. Cloud, Minnesota

Dedication

To my family who inspires me everyday,
and to my boys who truly embody
the characters of Joe-Joe and Biscuit.

Contents

Chapter 1   The Lions   1

Chapter 2   The Case   9

Chapter 3   Brutus and Betty Blue Beaver   19

Chapter 4   Candy Cardinal   27

Chapter 5   Liam the Llama   35

Chapter 6   Huckleberry Moose   45

Chapter 7   The Missing Mineral   55

Did You Know?   65

Some Terms to Identify Rocks and Minerals   67

Experiments   71

Rock Cycle   74

1
THE LIONS

"ROOAAR!" The scary sound of six lions, each the size of a motorcycle, filled the air. The lions began pacing the ground in front of Detective Joe-Joe Nut, one of the best detectives in Acorn Valley, trying to intimidate him. He was standing his ground though. Well, okay, it was more like his back was pressed up against a nearby wall in terror, but he looked brave on the outside. Being a squirrel, even a large one, he knew he didn't have a chance against these teenage lions if they decided to get rough with him. To them, he was an adult who appreciated authority and the respect of other animals. The young lions would have none of that. They stopped their pacing and loomed closer and closer until Joe-Joe could smell their breath drifting over him. The decaying smell of food could have choked an elephant. *Have we heard of a toothbrush?* thought Joe-Joe as he waved his paw in front of his nose, trying to clear the air.

Quickly, he gazed at the empty rows around him. He noticed right away some damaged equipment lying in pieces on the ground to the left of the lions. He shook his head in disgust, then looked up at the top of the circus tent, remembering how he had gotten himself

in this situation in the first place. It was because of a favor. Trouble always began with a favor. Here's the problem and how it all began.

These lions were bullies. Yes, and the worst kind. They were big kids who pushed around weaker or smaller animals to make themselves feel bigger and stronger. They jostled each other almost as much, too. After several days of being unruly in school, the lions finally got suspended for a few days by the principal. Since then they had been prowling around Acorn Valley, seeing who they could intimidate next. Joe-Joe's mother, Stella, had seen them chase Arsalean, a younger circus lion cub, into an empty circus tent. The circus animals had taken an early lunch after a strenuous morning practice. Stella hated injustice and mentioned to

"HAVE WE HEARD OF A TOOTHBRUSH?"

Joe-Joe that it wasn't the first time the gang of lions had been picking on Arsalean. The poor cub couldn't get a break.

Joe-Joe, along with his partner Biscuit Bill, had been visiting
Stella and eating lunch themselves when it all went down. Joe-Joe
was enraged with the rowdy lions' behavior, promising his mother
that he would handle it. Biscuit had urged Joe-Joe not to go by himself or to act too quickly. He said it wasn't a good idea. Biscuit had a
plan he thought would work against that particular bunch of willful
teenagers, but Joe-Joe didn't listen. He was fired up. He went off on
his own, and promptly found himself face to face with six very large
young lions. And, considering just how big and scary lions could
get, these six were not far from adult size.

The lions were not listening to anything he was saying, and Joe-
Joe felt he was soon to know what a ball of yarn felt like in the paws of
playful kittens. Only these kittens had huge claws and even bigger teeth.

Out of desperation, Joe-Joe had tried several tactics he thought
might diffuse the situation, might help him walk away in one piece. He
tried to be nice and kind, hoping to hit some inner goodness, but that
didn't work. The lions just narrowed their huge yellow eyes at him. He
then tried to use guilt, reminding them of the consequences of their
actions when destroying property, but that didn't work either. They just
showed their teeth in huge toothy smiles. He had tried puffing himself
up and acting the authority figure, but he had to dodge their enormous
paws when they laughed and tried to bat him around. Joe-Joe was out
of ideas and wasn't sure how things were going to turn out. All he knew
was Arsalean was safe. Wait, where was Arsalean?

Gazing behind the lions, Joe-Joe could see Arsalean on the other side of the arena. He was crouched down, obviously terrified, and holding something in his paw. It must have been what the lions were after. It was hard to see exactly what it was, but whatever it was, Arsalean obviously wanted it to have endured bullying while still keeping hold of his prize. All Joe-Joe could see was a dark blob. When Arsalean's paw shifted into the light, a part of the object shined brightly. It looked like Arsalean's lunch money. Yep, Arsalean probably got his lunch money taken from him every day, but had held onto it tight today. Realizing Joe-Joe was staring at him, Arsalean closed his paw self-consciously and held it to his golden chest. Before Joe-Joe could see more, a lion stepped in front of him, blocking his view of Arsalean. The lions began to roar loudly in unison.

Though Joe-Joe figured the six big lions were acting tough for show, he didn't want to test the theory. The largest lion of the group, a male with the beginnings of his full mane named Kojo, stepped forward and made the first move.

"You were foolish to intervene on Arsalean's behalf, Detective Nut."

Joe-Joe's eyes grew wide as he stared at Kojo, not remembering that his uniform probably gave him away—he did look professional.

"Yes, I know who you are. We all do. But your services are not needed here. My problem isn't with you. So you are free to go."

4

Kojo stepped back to let Joe-Joe move away from the wall. Joe-Joe knew they'd probably go after Arsalean as soon as he left and resolved he was going to protect Arsalean still, but, when he looked, the younger lion was nowhere to be seen. The lions looked as well, also noticing Arsalean's disappearance. Kojo roared loudly in anger, knowing his chance to bully Arsalean had passed, and turned once again on Joe-Joe.

"Let me at him," growled the lion just to Kojo's left. Joe-Joe figured he was going to have to fight his way out of this mess. He took an attack stance, raising his arms into his most threatening Kung Fu pose. Kojo took a deep breath and raised his paw to hold back his friend. When the lion proceeded to push passed Kojo, Kojo unexpectedly pounced on the lion, pressing his back into the dirt.

"No, leave him alone. I'm not going to jail for attacking a detective. That's just asking for trouble. Think about it, Rex. We're already in trouble because you broke that piece of equipment over there. You need to control your temper."

Kojo was smart, that was for sure, but why he and his buddies would bully other animals was beyond Joe-Joe's thinking. When Kojo let his friend up, he turned angrily toward Joe-Joe, but before any words could be said, a sound made them all turn to the entrance.

Biscuit Bill, his feathered wings folded in front of his chest, was flanked by two lions, but these weren't teenagers. One was Arsalean's father, Artemus, the lead trainer of the circus. He was enormous and had a huge mane of tawny hair. The other lion was Kojo's father, King, who owned the local football stadium, Forage Field,

and he was even bigger with a bristling mane of black hair. Neither lion looked the least amused. Kojo and his friends, who were actually his brothers, cringed. They might consider batting around a little squirrel, but they had no chance against their muscular, mighty, and very angry father.

"What is the meaning of this, boys?" King roared loudly.

Kojo looked at his brothers, then at his father. "Aw, Dad, were just having some fun. We weren't going to hurt any body."

"Fun? You were having some fun?" King raised his enormous paws to his head for a second, then regained his composure. "I received a call from your principal about bullying other students and being suspended from school. I hear from Detective Bill that you've been bullying Arsalean nearly every day. That is going to stop as of right now. Then you come into the circus tent and damage property?" King pointed a paw towards the broken equipment on the ground. "That was expensive. Does that sound like fun to you now?"

Kojo and his brothers bowed their heads in shame, not being able to reply.

"I know I work long hours and don't spend enough time with you at home as I'd like, but this is no way to behave. You six will be paying for the damaged equipment, not me."

Kojo looked up at his father and then glared at Rex, knowing he was responsible for the damage.

Artemus, Arsalean's dad, said, "King, I have an idea on how the boys can repay me for the damage."

King looked at Artemus. "I'm open to any ideas you may have, Artemus. In fact, because they damaged your property, you should be the one to come up with the proper punishment for them."

Seeing that the fathers had the situation under control, Biscuit and Joe-Joe left them to it and headed for their white van parked just outside the tent. As they pulled out onto the street, they quickly came to Joe-Joe's mom's house. She waved at them from her window as they drove passed. Joe-Joe blew her a kiss. He then sat back in his seat, adjusted the seatbelt over his shoulder, and asked Biscuit, "How did you . . ." He was still trying to figure out how Biscuit got King and Artemus together so quickly.

"I told you I had a plan, but you didn't listen. I knew King and Artemus were friends. They meet every Tuesday at eleven for lunch to talk about any upcoming circus events and football games. And, today is Tuesday."

Joe-Joe nodded, then shook his head sadly, alarmed by his foolishness. The situation could have ended badly. Thank goodness it didn't.

"Never put yourself into a situation where you're outnumbered. You know that, Joe-Joe. You certainly shouldn't have tried to handle the situation on your own. We're partners. We should've handled this situation together. You let your mom emotionally side track you. It takes the two of us to make things work, two of us to protect each other, especially when bullies are around. Neither of us are very big. We have to watch out for tough situations and realize that we can't always handle things on our own. We must ask for help, sometimes."

7

"Yes, yes. I know you're right, Biscuit. Thanks for helping me. Actually, I learned a lot from this experience. I won't ever try to solve this kind of thing again by myself." Joe-Joe turned to look out the window.

Biscuit chuckled. "By the way, was that Kung Fu you were going to use on Rex if he attacked you? Impressive. I was almost going to wait and see that show," teased Biscuit.

Joe-Joe began to laugh too. "It would've been a short one, believe me. My Kung Fu's rusty."

Joe-Joe and Biscuit were laughing together when they heard a voice flow from their police radio. Dispatch was trying to get hold of them. Joe-Joe cleared his throat and reached for the radio. In a serious, calm voice he responded. "This is Joe-Joe, Dispatch."

"We just received a call from Melinda Moo. Something's been stolen. You and Biscuit need to get over there as soon as possible. I'm sending the location to your GPS."

"It's probably these lion brother's," commented Joe-Joe softly to Biscuit before replying to Dispatch more loudly. "Thanks! We're heading there now." He then returned the radio mic back to its holder on the dashboard and leaned back. He glanced at their GPS screen toward the center of the van and saw the downloaded directions already up. After taking several deep breaths, he focused his attention on the farm fields around them.

2
THE CASE

It was a beautiful summer's day. The sun shone brightly, which caused Joe-Joe and Biscuit to put on their black sunglasses, which matched their sleek black suits. The air was clean and crisp. Joe-Joe rolled down his window to feel the breeze wash over him as they drove to the other side of town. Before he knew it, Biscuit had pulled into Melinda Moo's driveway. The house looked very much like a barn with its tall roof and sliding front door. Joe-Joe made sure he had his notepad and pencil before stepping out of the van and meeting up with Biscuit, who had already knocked on the door.

It didn't take long for the door to open. Standing there in the doorway was a tall tan cow. She was wearing a long forest green, dress with white trim around the sleeves. Lying loosely around her large neck hung a beautiful salmon colored pearl necklace.

"Good morning, ma'am. I'm Detective Biscuit Bill and this is my partner, Detective Joe-Joe Nut. We received a call that you had something stolen?"

Melinda Moo looked like she was trying to remain cool and calm, but failing miserably. In fact, she looked very upset and on the

verge of tears. "I'm glad you're here. Please, come in." She moved aside to allow Joe-Joe and Biscuit to enter.

The inside of Melinda Moo's house was extremely clean and well kept. She led Joe-Joe and Biscuit into the living room so they could sit down on a large russet-brown sofa, then offered them some tea, which they both accepted. Serving tea seemed to calm her. When Melinda was finally ready to talk, she sat down in a chair across from them. She held her head high, took a deep breath, and began. "My daughter collects rocks and minerals, you see, and one of her favorite minerals was stolen from her collection."

Joe-Joe leaned forward and whispered, "It wasn't a group of lion brothers was it?"

"What? No!" Melinda glanced at Biscuit, her eyes flying open, wondering what in the world he was talking about.

Biscuit gave Joe-Joe a look to drop the lion discussion so Melinda didn't get too upset. Joe-Joe lowered his head, focusing his attention on his notepad. Biscuit glanced over at what he wrote. In large letters, Joe-Joe had scribbled, "NOT THE LION BROTH-ERS!" Biscuit returned his attention to Melinda Moo.

"What kind of mineral was it, ma'am?" asked Biscuit. Before Melinda could answer, Joe-Joe added, "And what makes it so valuable? I mean, most rocks and minerals are just—"

"I know what you must be thinking, detectives," interrupted Melinda. "Most collections aren't worth much. I can see where you are going with this, Detective Nut, and I understand your hesitation

on the matter. You think I'm worked up about some meaningless rock in an ordinary collection. I assure you, I'm not wasting your time."

Joe-Joe smiled sweetly, still having his doubts, but saying nothing further.

"Most youngsters collect your basic rocks and minerals, such as quartz, pyrite, geodes, and sandstone, but my daughter's collection is filled with more unique rocks and minerals than that." Melinda took a deep breath and placed a hoof on her chest. "The most valuable mineral she has came from a gem mine in California. It was a combination of benitoite and neptunite minerals."

"What and what?" asked Joe-Joe, not familiar at all with those two types of minerals. Before Melinda could answer, Biscuit reached into his jacket pocket, where he kept everything he could possibly need on a case, and pulled out a rock and mineral book. This pocket was no ordinary pocket, though Biscuit didn't talk about it much. It was a magic pocket that could produce items he needed on demand.

"Benitoite and neptunite," repeated Biscuit as he flipped through the pages. "Well, let's see. When dealing with minerals, one must always keep in mind its physical characteristics or properties, such as color, luster, transparency, hardness, streak, fracture, cleavage, and specific gravity. These characteristics are unique identifiers for each mineral." Biscuit flipped through the pages. "Now, neptunite is a rare mineral and can be found in combination with benitoite. Neptunite has an internal red reflection, but is sometimes red and black on the outside, while benitoite has a sapphire-blue color." Biscuit

closed the book and placed it back into his jacket pocket. "Miss Moo, what is the value of this particular mineral?"

Melinda lowered her hoof from her chest and gazed intently at Biscuit and Joe-Joe. "It's worth thousands."

"Of dollars?" squeaked Joe-Joe unbelievably.

Melinda couldn't resist, "No, Detective Nut, it's worth thousands of sea shells." Melinda shook her head, her sarcasm filling the air like a stinky sock after a basketball game. "Of course dollars!" she snapped. Melinda's carefully groomed hair suddenly fell over her eyes, her cheeks becoming rosy.

Joe-Joe nearly fell from his seat on the sofa.

Biscuit cleared his throat, remaining calm despite the tension-filled room. He'd an idea of the mineral's worth when he had read the words "rare" under the description, but he had to ask. "I thought as much. I can see why you called us in to investigate."

Biscuit stood up. Joe-Joe did the same, fixing his tie and straightening his suit as he did. "We'll need to see where your daughter kept the mineral and to speak with her, if possible."

"Of course, detective. Please, right this way." Melinda stood, her composure returning as she led the detectives to a room towards the back of the barn. The door was shut, but Melinda knocked briefly before sliding it open. Inside was a medium-sized calf wearing a bright pink dress with her hair in pigtails. Lining the wall of her room were shelves filled with various types of minerals, many in small boxes to protect them. One box appeared to be empty.

MAPLE AND MELINDA MOO

"Maple, these are detectives Joe-Joe Nut and Biscuit Bill. They're here to help us find your missing mineral, so please cooperate."

Maple nodded and approached Biscuit and Joe-Joe. "Hello, detectives."

"Good morning, Maple. Was this where your missing mineral was kept?" asked Biscuit as he pointed towards the empty box.

"Yes, it was."

"Who had access to your collection?" asked Joe-Joe.

"The mineral was in my room yesterday before my friends came over, but after they left, it was gone. I already asked them, but they all denied taking it. I felt bad even asking, to be honest, but it had to have gone somewhere. It wouldn't have just grown legs and walked away."

"Could you have misplaced it? You know, like maybe you were showing your friends the mineral and set it down, got distracted, and then left it in an unusual place?" asked Joe-Joe. "I get distracted all the time," he added. "It's like, look over there, something shiny, and off I go."

Maple looked at Joe-Joe strangely, as if that had never happened to her before.

"No, I didn't do anything like that, detective. In fact, I never lifted the box or took the mineral out of it. The box was in the exact location it is now. My friends saw my rare mineral through its clear casing, but no one touched it, at least that I saw, and I was being pretty observant, I thought."

"Well, someone definitely touched it," muttered Joe-Joe as he wrote down some information on his notepad. Biscuit stepped closer to the box on the shelf. Not being able to reach it, he moved over a nearby stool. He took a measuring tape from his magic pocket and measured it's height, which was twelve inches tall, then studied it for clues. After that, he stepped onto it. He studied the box for sev-

eral minutes before touching it. There were no scratch marks on the box or prints. It was not damaged in any way. No lingering drool clouded the clear lid. Biscuit took down the box and put it on Maple's desk. He then began to measure the height from the shelf to the floor. What concerned him was the fact that the shelf was

MAPLE MOO'S MISSING MINERAL

around six feet high on the wall, about seventy-two inches from the floor. He gave that information to Joe-Joe, who wrote it on his notepad, trying to keep up with Biscuit's measurements.

Biscuit returned the box to its place on the high shelf. "Can you tell me the names of your friends, so we can question them?" asked Biscuit as he stepped down from the stool and walked back over to stand beside his partner.

"Sure! There was Brutus and Betty Blue Beaver— they are twins. Then there was Candy Cardinal, Liam the Llama, and Huckleberry Moose. We all collect rocks. We have lots in common with each other because of that."

Joe-Joe wrote down the names.

"Do you have a picture of your missing mineral?"

Maple nodded and retrieved a picture from the photo album she kept of all her rocks and minerals. She showed it to Biscuit.

Biscuit said, "Could I borrow this for a little while?"

"I guess so," Maple said.

Biscuit put the picture into his pocket.

"Do your friends have photo albums of their rock collections as well?" asked Joe-Joe.

"Huck does. I've seen it. He has some really nice specimens, too. He gets one really nice rock or mineral a year to add to his collection. Huck's dad is a geologist, so he's found some pretty nice rocks over the years. Huck's not allowed to handle them much, though. He collects sedimentary rock, so some specimens are pretty

fragile. He uses cases just like mine, too. His dad's really strict on that, but his mom would rather toss the whole collection out. She's not into rocks and doesn't understand our love of them."

"What about the others?" asked Biscuit.

"Liam collects various kinds of rocks. His favorites are volcanic rocks. He loves volcanoes. He's full of information, just ask him. Brutus and Betty Blue like various minerals. Their quartz collection is rather impressive. Candy loves things that are shiny. She collects minerals as well, but mostly gemstones. She likes to make jewelry."

Joe-Joe scribbled all the information down on his notepad.

"What is the estimated size of your missing mineral?" asked Biscuit. "So we have something to compare it too."

"Well, the overall size is eleven by eight by three centimeters. The sizes of the individual crystals are around three to eighteen millimeters." Biscuit reached into his jacket pocket and pulled out a ruler. The ruler contained both millimeter and centimeter measurements. After looking at it several times, he whispered to Joe-Joe, and had him write down the important information. He gave him the ruler to draw a box the size of the mineral as reference. He then tucked the ruler back into his magic jacket pocket.

"Very good," Biscuit said. "You gave us tons of information to work with. Detective Joe-Joe and I will be keeping in touch. Thank you for your time, Maple."

Biscuit then turned to Melinda, who was standing in the doorway. "Miss Moo, don't worry. We're on the case. Your daughter

will get her crystal back in no time." Joe-Joe and Biscuit smiled re-assuringly before walking out of Maple's room, through the barn and out the front door, where their van awaited to take them to seek out their first suspect.

3
BRUTUS AND BETTY BLUE BEAVER

In the van, Joe-Joe sat in the passenger seat, reading the rock and mineral book that Biscuit had given him. Knowing very little about

these things, he wanted to study up before meeting each suspect. In all honesty, Joe-Joe wasn't interested in rocks and minerals. In fact, he thought they were pretty boring. Biscuit looked over at Joe-Joe, who was now staring out the window.

"What's wrong, Joe-Joe?"

"I just don't get the fascination with collecting rocks and minerals. I mean, they're rocks. We walk on them all the time and crush them beneath our feet. What's the big deal?"

"Did you collect anything when you were a youngster?"

Joe-Joe thought about it for a minute, then smiled. "Actually, I did. I collected nuts. Not just acorns either, but various kinds of nuts. Whenever we went on vacation, I would bring home a new kind of nut and add it to my collection. I even labeled them and everything, kept them in cases, too. I've lost a few over the years,

though. Some became trees in our backyard. Mother always wondered why a species of tree not native to our surroundings would suddenly start growing in our yard. I'd nuture it until it grew big and strong. Those trees had provided us with nuts for years. I loved collecting nuts. I knew everything about them, too."

Biscuit smiled. "How many did you have in your collection?"

"Oh—around a hundred and forty."

Biscuit shook his head. "You know, some animals might think that collecting nuts would be boring. A nut is just a nut, isn't it? I mean, if you've seen one, you've probably seen them all."

Joe-Joe shook his head, ready to defend his nut collection. "No! Each nut is unique in what it looks like and how it develops. It is actually a seed, and …" Joe-Joe paused and nodded his head, realizing what Biscuit was doing. "I get it, Biscuit. You're saying that no collection is pointless to the collector. I loved collecting nuts. These animals like to collect rocks and minerals. I shouldn't be so judgmental."

Biscuit hadn't said a word, but his grin indicated he was glad that Joe-Joe understood where he was going with the topic.

"Give rocks and minerals a chance, Joe-Joe. Just like your nut collection, you had as a kid, you might find them interesting and worthwhile once this case is over. You may just begin to understand why these animals love to collect them so much." Joe-Joe nodded his head, willing to be open to the possibility.

Joe-Joe was ready to agree. "All right, I'll give rocks and minerals a chance. I won't be so negative."

"Thanks, Joe-Joe. That's all I'm asking."

Joe-Joe and Biscuit made their way to their first suspect. Brutus and Betty Blue lived at the edge of the valley. Their house was made of logs and was located in the center of a pond. As they pulled up, they saw a small paddle boat by the pond's edge. As it was the only way to the Beaver house, they got in. Each grabbed an oar and paddled themselves to the beaver's dock. When the boat was tied, Joe-Joe and Biscuit knocked on the front door.

Soon the door opened to reveal an adult beaver with glasses. "Yes, can I help you?" the beaver asked as he held onto the day's paper.

"I'm Detective Biscuit Bill and this is my partner, Detective Joe-Joe Nut. We're investigating the case of a missing mineral. Is Brutus or Betty Blue around, sir?"

**JOE-JOE & BISCUIT
QUESTION THE BEAVER FAMILY**

Mr. Beaver glanced behind him at Brutus and Betty Blue who were playing with their rock collection on the floor. "Please come in, detectives."

"Thank you, sir," replied Joe-Joe as they entered the house. The floor was covered with rugs. Pictures of the family hung on the log walls of the living room. Brutus and Betty Blue were twins. Betty Blue wore a soft baby pink dress and pretty bow, while Brutus wore a light tan shirt that matched nicely with his dark navy blue pants.

"You want to talk to us?" asked Betty Blue as she stood away from her collection. She seemed particularly excited for the attention and focus.

"Yes, Betty Blue, I do," said Biscuit. "Do you happen to know why?"

Betty Blue shook her small brown head.

"Well," continued Biscuit softly. "There's a mineral missing from Maple Moo's collection. It disappeared this morning from the Moo house. Do you know anything about it?"

Betty Blue shook her head, her features filled with surprise. Biscuit quickly turned to Brutus, who was already shaking his head.

"Which mineral was taken?" he asked.

"The benitoite and neptunite mineral," replied Biscuit, and he took out the picture of the mineral and showed everyone.

Brutus's eyes lit up. "Maple showed us that mineral this morning. It's an amazing combination. We were really impressed by its beauty. It's quite rare you know."

"We know," said Joe-Joe, watching the twins. "What do you know about it?"

"Not much . . . really, just what Maple told us. She showed the mineral to us when we were in her room. We couldn't touch it or anything, so we couldn't really get a good look at it, but we respect that. We know it's valuable. We collect minerals ourselves, so we'd heard about those two types of minerals, but to be honest, I would've been afraid to touch it. It's too rare."

"Would you mind us looking at your collection?" asked Biscuit.

"No, not at all, sir," answered Brutus, brightening. As he stood up next to his sister, Joe-Joe noticed they were same height.

"How tall are the two of you?" Joe-Joe asked casually, his notepad open and pencil in paw.

"We're twenty-eight inches," said Betty Blue proudly. "We're twins, so we're the same size."

Joe-Joe nodded as he wrote. "How were you able to see the mineral then? You certainly are not tall enough?"

"Our friend Liam let us climb onto his back," replied Brutus. "He's a llama and was tall enough to view the mineral without help."

"Hmmm," said Joe-Joe as he wrote on his notepad.

"Is this all of your collection?" asked Biscuit as he pointed to the rocks on the floor.

"Yes, sir, it is," answered Betty Blue.

"It's rather impressive. I see quartz here. Can you tell us about some of them?"

"Sure!" answered the twins, their faces lighting up with excitement. "What do you want to know?"

"Tell us about some of the big ones," said Biscuit as he pointed his wing at a bright purple specimen.

"Do you know much about quartz?" asked Brutus.

"Some."

"Well, we collect quartz. Our specimens are mostly in their original form, nothing polished, except for Betty Blue's rose quartz over there. It's in the shape of an elephant." Betty Blue picked up the rose quartz and showed it to Joe-Joe and Biscuit proudly.

"We collect various types of rock crystals, which is sometimes called clear quartz. It's called that because you can see right through it. We have some of the colored varieties as well, like citrine, amethyst, and smoky quartz, and we also have quite a few others that you have probably heard of too. We have agate, onyx, jasper, aventurine, tigers' eye, and chalcedony."

Out of all the beautiful specimens that Biscuit and Joe-Joe saw, none were blue or even came close in color to Maple's missing mineral.

"Thank you so much for sharing your collection with us," said Joe-Joe to Brutus and Betty Blue.

"Anytime, detective. I hope you find Maple's mineral. It's really a treasure. She must be very upset." Betty Blue turned to her brother. "Maybe we should go over there and see how she's doing?"

Brutus and Betty Blue looked at their father. He popped his head up from his paper, and Joe-Joe saw his large teeth that he had used to build his handsome home. Father Beaver nodded.

"We can go over there and see her in a few minutes." Mr. Beaver then turned towards Joe-Joe and Biscuit. He walked them to the door while his offspring ran to their rooms to get ready. "If we run across the missing mineral, we'll certainly let you know, detectives. I checked their collection as soon as I heard that Maple had lost one. I didn't see her mineral among them. That doesn't mean that it wasn't hidden somewhere, though I doubt my twins took it on purpose. I'll be checking their collection again as soon as you leave," Mr. Beaver assured them.

Biscuit removed a business card from his pocket. "Well, if something shows up, my number's on the card. Give me a call."

"WELL, IF SOMETHING COMES UP, MY NUMBERS ON THE CARD."

"Thank you, detectives, I will."

Joe-Joe and Biscuit walked out the front door and back to the boat, where they rowed to shore. Back in their van, they were soon on their way to question the next suspect.

4
CANDY CARDINAL

Candy Cardinal lived in a tall full-sized pine tree with her family not far from the beaver pond. Her house was tiny, but it was decorated nicely on the outside with several flower boxes by the windows and was perched on some pine needles. Biscuit reached up and knocked on the small green door with his wing.

A small brownish-red bird answered the door. "Hello!"

"Are you Candy Cardinal?" asked Biscuit.

"Yes. What can I do for you?"

"I'm Detective Biscuit Bill and this is my partner, Detective Joe-Joe Nut. We're investigating the case of a missing mineral. Do you know anything about a missing mineral?"

Candy shrugged her small shoulders and shook her head. "I don't know anything about a missing mineral, detective. Whose mineral is missing, if you don't mind me asking?"

"Maple Moo's," replied Joe-Joe.

Candy took a slight intake of breath and raised her wing to her beak.

"Which one?" she asked hesitantly, looking scared.

"The benitoite and neptunite mineral."

Candy's eyes grew even larger as she shook her head again. "That's Maple's pride and joy. It's such a unique and rare mineral, and expensive. I can't believe someone took it."

"DO YOU LIKE MY NECKLACE?"

"Neither can we," said Joe-Joe as he glanced at his notepad and pencil. "Because you were over at Maple's house before the mineral was stolen this morning, we must ask you a few questions."

"Of course, detective. I'll help if I can," said Candy.

"Thank you, Candy. First, how tall are you?"

"Oh, I'm around five inches tall, but that doesn't include my lovely tail."

"Indeed. What kinds of rocks or minerals do you collect?" continued Joe-Joe.

"I do collect some minerals, mostly small decorative gemstones. I make jewelry. Do you like my necklace?" Candy stepped further onto her porch so they could get a closer look. Biscuit and Joe-Joe leaned closer to see the bright red stones on her necklace.

"Those are beautiful, Candy. What kind of gem is that?" asked Joe-Joe.

"These are all rubies," replied Candy proudly.

"You said you made the necklace yourself?" asked Biscuit, fingering the stones appreciatively.

"Yes! I have a passion for making jewelry."

"Is it possible for us to see your full collection?" continued Biscuit eagerly.

"Okay, if you could wait here for a minute. I'll go and get it." Candy turned around and half-hopped and half-flew her way inside her house. Within minutes, Candy returned with her wing and beak

pulling on a cloth sac. Biscuit reached up and over to open the sac. Inside were several small polished gemstones.

"Can you tell us about some of these?" asked Biscuit.

"Sure! Notice that most of my gemstones are broken up and polished. I have no minerals in their raw form. To be honest, those aren't nearly as pretty. Regular rocks are boring, but when they're broken up and polished, their beauty can be truly inspiring. Do you know much about gemstones, detectives?" asked Candy.

"Their pretty. That's the extent of my knowledge," replied Joe-Joe candidly. Biscuit glanced over at his partner and shook his head. He then focused his attention back on Candy.

"I'm familiar with rocks and minerals to a degree, but could you tell us more about them?" said Biscuit.

"Of course! Let's see, where to begin? Oh, I know something that might interest you. Gemstones have some pretty fascinating histories. Each gemstone has a particular color and properties, but some also have myths or legends about them."

"Really?" whispered Biscuit. "I didn't know that."

"Yep!" Candy glanced around in her collection and pulled out a shiny smooth black rock with her wing. "We'll use this piece of onyx as an example. Onyx is the birthstone for December and for the zodiac sign Leo. Now, black onyx is a chalcedony quartz that is mined in various places around the world. It can come in different colors other than black, too. There's also a Greek legend about it. The legend says that one day while Venus, also known as Aphrodite,

was sleeping, Eros cut her fingernails and left the clippings on the ground. The gods turned them into stones which later became known as onyx. It's also said that it has healing properties. It can help with happiness, intuition, and helps stop bad habits. I'll admit it helped me stop biting my claws."

"Maybe I should get one," added Joe-Joe as he thought of a few bad habits he would like to break.

"How do you know so much about the onyx?" asked Biscuit.

"Lots of research, of course. I've looked up the histories of all my gemstones. It also helps that my father's a gemologist." She puffed up her feathers. "He's a certified professional who identifies, grades and appraises gemstones. He knows a lot of stuff and works closely with the jeweler in town. He also uses tons of big words. I have a hard time pronouncing some of them," added Candy.

"What are some of the other minerals you have in your collection?" asked Joe-Joe.

"Oh, obviously I have onyx, but I also have ruby, jasper, rose quartz, moss agate, lace agate, amethyst, quartz, turquoise, hematite, malachite, and some snowflake obsidian." Biscuit had his attention focused on a shiny mineral kept in a clear case.

"And that one, Candy. I'm curious about that one."

Again she fluffed her feathers. "You're referring to my most prized possession. This, detectives, is a diamond. I found it lying in the dirt near the mountains. Knowing its worth, I keep it in a case to protect it." Joe-Joe was writing on his notepad frantically

"ARE YOU OKAY DOWN THERE?"

throughout Candy's speech. When she was finished, he glanced at Biscuit and shook his head.

"With our years of experience as detectives, sometimes looks can be deceiving. Would you indulge us in an experiment to prove your innocence of the matter?"

"Sure. What kind of experiment?" asked Candy.

Biscuit pulled out a mineral from his pocket.

"From my estimation, this is a mineral similar to the weight of Maple's missing one. We're going to have you pick it up and carry it." Biscuit set it on top of Candy's porch and watched as she hopped and flew on top of it.

"Let me know when you're ready, detectives."

"Go!" commanded Biscuit. Candy flapped her wings as fast as she could. Her face began to change to a deeper red as she lifted

the mineral and began to fly towards Biscuit. The flight lasted only a few seconds before Candy and the mineral dropped to the ground faster than a pinecone from her pine tree. She was exhausted. Biscuit and Joe-Joe both looked down at their feet and saw Candy's fast panting as she fanned her face with her wing.

"That works for me. How about you, Joe-Joe? Need any more proof?"

"Nope, I'm good." Joe-Joe then looked down at his feet. "Are you okay down there?" Joe-Joe reached down and picked up Candy, lifting her to stand on her porch.

"Yes, detective! Was that proof enough that I couldn't have committed the crime?"

Joe-Joe and Biscuit both nodded their heads. "You're free to go," said Biscuit as he pulled out a business card from his pocket and handed it to Candy. "If you hear anything, please let us know."

"I will, detective," replied Candy as she placed the card on top of her rock sac and pulled the load back towards her house.

Joe-Joe and Biscuit began to walk back towards their van. Once inside, Joe-Joe glanced over his notes.

"Okay, so far we have three suspects who couldn't have committed the crime."

"Well," began Biscuit, "let's go over what we know."

"The Beaver twins aren't tall enough to grab the mineral off of Maple's shelf by themselves. They admitted having to stand on Liam's back to see it in the first place."

"Well, they could've used Maple's stool like I did . . . while standing on each other's head," pointed out Biscuit.

"True, but they don't have the stolen mineral in their collection or even collect that kind of mineral to begin with. They collect quartz. Why would they steal something else? They'd have no use for it, and it'd surely stand out when their father checked."

"Good point," said Biscuit. "Next suspect."

"Candy Cardinal just proved that she couldn't have flown home with the mineral. It would've been way too heavy for her. Plus, there were no scratch marks on the case showing that she even attempted to lift it, and she would have had too, again, unless she had help."

Biscuit raised his wing to his face and tapped his chin.

Joe-Joe continued. "Candy also collects gemstones for making jewelry. She'd have no use for Maple's mineral. Plus, her father's a gemologist, and I'm sure he can provide her with whatever mineral she wanted. She has a diamond in her collection, for goodness sakes. Why steal someone else's mineral?"

Biscuit nodded in agreement as he started the van.

"I believe we should be off to visit our next suspect. I hope Liam has more information to help us with this case, because of right now, we have nothing," said Biscuit.

5
LIAM THE LLAMA

 The detectives drove a few miles from Candy Cardinal's pine tree to question their next suspect. Liam the Llama lived in a wooden house near a pasture of tall grasses with his family and siblings. A few of the llama family were in the pasture playing touch football when Joe-Joe and Biscuit drove up. Biscuit recognized the father because he was Acorn Valley High's football coach. Joe-Joe and Biscuit had both been to some of the games. They were in a winning season so far, with only three losses. Coach Llama was in the field running plays and blowing whistles. Not only were some of his llama children playing football, but a few alligators, a zebra, two horses, an elephant—who was very hard to block—and a buffalo.

Biscuit and Joe-Joe stepped out of the van and walked towards the field. Coach Llama had just blown a rather loud whistle when he noticed them. "Hey, folks. Can I help you?"

"Yes, sir. I'm Biscuit Bill and this is my partner, Joe-Joe Nut. We're detectives on the case of a missing mineral. We would like to speak with your son, Liam. Is he around?" Coach Llama glanced towards his field of players, then back at the detectives. Before Coach could speak, an

explosion shook the house. A second-floor window was immediately opened, and black smoke billowed briefly. A hoof waved the smoke out. Coach Llama shook his head and took a deep breath.

"Liam's inside, apparently playing with his volcano again."

"Excuse me?" said Joe-Joe.

BEFORE COACH COULD SPEAK,
AN EXPLOSION CAME FROM THE HOUSE

"He's constructing a working model of an erupting volcano for the science fair at school. He's fascinated by volcanoes."

"Thank you, sir," said Joe-Joe before Coach Llama blew his whistle and turned around towards the teams in front of him, yelling the next play. Biscuit and Joe-Joe shook their heads as they walked towards the house. Biscuit knocked on the door while Joe-Joe flipped to an empty page on his notepad. When the door opened, a dirt-covered Liam answered the door. His wool, already a dark brown, appeared black from the dirt and maybe a little singed about his head. Smoke billowed out the door past his head. Being a llama, he stood taller than both Joe-Joe and Biscuit.

"Yes!" spouted a disgruntled Liam. He blinked, looked around and coughed.

"Are you Liam?" asked Biscuit.

Liam looked down at Joe-Joe and Biscuit. "Y-e-s?" Liam replied a little more hesitantly.

"Detective Biscuit Bill here and my partner, Detective Joe-Joe Nut. We're investigating a case of a missing mineral. Do you know anything about such a thing?"

"I don't know. Who's missing their mineral?" asked Liam.

"Maple Moo! She's missing her benitoite and neptunite mineral," answered Joe-Joe.

Liam's eyes grew wide. "Really? I was over her house this morning with some friends. Is that when it happened?" Now concern filled Liam's dirty features. He scratched a smoking ear.

"The mineral disappeared some time during your visit or just after you and your friends left," answered Joe-Joe.

Liam turned his head and appeared to be thinking about something for several minutes. Then his focus returned to the detectives in front of him. "Okay, but what do you want to see me for?"

"Since you were over at Maple's house this morning, we need to question you about the mineral's disappearance. It's standard procedure," spoke Biscuit, already realizing that Liam was distracted.

"Of course—yes."

Biscuit glanced skeptically at Liam. "What do you know about the mineral?"

"Not much. Only what Maple told us. The others seemed to know more about the mineral than I did, since some of them collect minerals. I don't. I collect volcanic rocks. Don't get me wrong, the mineral was pretty and all, but I was more interested in Maple's scrapbook of her minerals. She did a great job taking pictures of them. I want to start one for my rocks. She was showing me how she did it." Joe-Joe wrote down Liam's answers.

"Can we see your collection of rocks?" asked Joe-Joe.

"Sure. Please, come in." Liam allowed the detectives to enter the house. He led them past the kitchen where there were two types of volcanoes sitting on lots of newspaper on top of his kitchen table. The first volcano was small and decoratively painted. A little bit of smoke still billowed from its top. The other volcano was a cross-section of a volcano. It was labeled and colored accordingly.

"I apologize for the mess. I'm working on my entry for the upcoming science fair at school." He then smiled and led the detectives into the living room where his rock collection was spread out on a table. He also had several books opened. When Joe-Joe glanced at the books, he noticed that they were all about volcanoes. He quickly wrote the information down on his notepad.

"Is this your complete rock collection?" asked Biscuit.

"Yup, all of it. Most of my collection consists of igneous rock, which is volcanic rock." Liam had some impressive specimens in his collection, but all were common rocks. Nothing rare.

"Can you tell us about some of these?" asked Joe-Joe.

"Sure. I have various types of volcanic rock in my collection. Some are either intrusive or extrusive rock." Liam bent down and picked up a few rocks on the table.

"What does that mean?" asked Joe-Joe.

"Well, intrusive rocks have a coarse grain, which means that their individual crystals are large and can be seen very clearly interlocked together. I have some great examples for you to see. I have granite, diorite, gabbro, and peridotite." Liam handed the rocks to Biscuit and Joe-Joe, who analyzed them. They could see the coarse grain of each rock and could feel their weight and roughness. After several minutes of studying the rocks, they gave them back to Liam who put them back onto the table. He then picked up a few others.

"Extrusive rocks have a finer grain, which means their crystals are smaller, harder to see. I have here rhyolite, andesite, basalt,

and komatiite. You should be able to see the fine grain clearly in these rocks. There's a big difference between the two kinds of rocks, if you compare them." Liam handed the rocks to the detectives. As they looked at them closely, they could see the fine grain of each rock. Biscuit bent over and picked up gabbro from the table and compared it to basalt.

"I do see a difference. That's amazing."

"I don't get it," stated Joe-Joe.

"What don't you get, detective?" asked Liam calmly. He could talk about volcanic rocks all day.

"I don't understand why some of these rocks have a fine or coarse grain. What determines that?"

"That's an excellent question, detective. Intrusive rocks cool differently than extrusive. The cooling of magma deep in the Earth is typically slower than it would be if it were at the surface, so large crystals form, creating an intrusive rock. For extrusive rocks, the magma cools rapidly at or near the surface not allowing any time for large crystals to form. Hence, the fine grain. Does that make sense now?"

"That's so interesting," began Joe-Joe, "that the grain of these rocks was determined by how quickly or how slowly magma cooled. You know, that's really neat. I didn't know that."

"I agree," said Biscuit. "Thank you for the science lesson, Liam." They each returned the rocks to Liam, who again placed them on the table. Biscuit dusted his wings off. As he did, he noticed

a cup of water on the table. The water had specs of rock in it so he knew it wasn't for drinking. "What's the cup of water for?"

"I was playing around with some rocks and doing some mini experiments. I love this experiment. It's so cool to see. Here, watch. As you can tell, I have no rare rocks in my collection. They're all pretty common in appearance—but not in their abilities. One of my favorite rocks is pumice." Liam picked up a large white rock. It was unique in appearance and had lots of holes in it. It looked almost like hardened foam or, to Joe-Joe, like a mass of melted marshmallows. Liam handed Biscuit the rock. It was extremely light and airy.

A ROCK THAT FLOATS!

"Now, volcanic rocks often have small cavities in them, and I don't mean like the ones the dentist finds. The cavities I'm talking about are holes. They're formed by the expansion of bubbles of gas or steam during the hardening of the rock. Pumice is an example of what an explosive volcanic eruption looks like. It has so many cavities that it can do something special."

Joe-Joe raised an eyebrow in curiosity. Liam took back the rock and dropped it in the cup of water. Most rocks would have sunk to the bottom of the cup, but the pumice floated calmly on top.

"Cool!" spouted Joe-Joe.

"Yeah, I think so, too," added Liam as he removed the pumice from the cup of water and placed it on a nearby towel to dry out.

"You know quite a bit about volcanic rocks," said Biscuit.

"I want to be a volcanologist one day. I love studying rocks. Very few colleges offer volcanology, though, so I'll have to major in geology. My dad doesn't approve of my choice. He'd rather I play football like my brothers, but I'm just not interested in sports. I'm trying to save up for a conference in a few months about geology at Antelope Plains."

"How much does it cost?"

"A couple hundred dollars. Dad won't pay for it, so I have to earn the money by mowing grass. It's a hard job because I can only mow so many yards a day before I get too full." Biscuit stared at Liam for several minutes—speechless. After watching Liam glance quickly at the watch on his foreleg and appearing a bit antsy, Joe-Joe reached into his jacket pocket and pulled out a business card, handing it to Liam.

"Well, until we solve this case, don't leave town. If you hear of anything, please give us a call."

"I will, detectives. I hope you catch the animal who took Maple's mineral."

Before Biscuit could open his mouth to protest, Joe-Joe placed his notepad and pencil into his pocket. He latched onto Biscuit's arm, pulling him toward the front door.

When the pair reached the side of the house away from Coach Llama's view, Biscuit turned on Joe-Joe faster than a snake

"WE ARE GOING TO LET HIM LEAD US TO WHOMEVER HE IS TRYING TO PROTECT."

attacking an intruder. "Why did you ease up? Liam's smart, but not enough to hide his impatience on wanting us to leave. He was up to something."

"I know!" spouted Joe-Joe as he raised his arm.

"What?" Biscuits eyes were large and bulging. Before any-more words could be said, they saw Liam sneak out a side door, glance several times to the right and left, then head into the woods.

"We're going to let him lead us to whomever he's trying to protect," began Joe-Joe. "Liam didn't commit the crime. I can about guarantee that, though needing money for his trip is motive. And he's the right height. I didn't have to ask him that. It was obvious he was tall enough to commit the crime. But, I'll bet you a bucket of acorns that he knows who did."

Biscuit was shocked at first, then smiled. "Good work, Joe-Joe. Let's follow him and see if he'll lead us to Huckleberry Moose."

6
HUCKLEBERRY MOOSE

Huckleberry Moose lived at the edge of the dense forest near a bog a mile away from Liam. His house was made from various trees and was huge in size. The landscape was filled with plants and flowers of all different kinds as well as tall conifer trees and some maples. The road Joe-Joe and Biscuit drove went around the forest. Needless to say, Liam beat them to Huckleberry's house. When they pulled up, all was quiet. Joe-Joe and Biscuit stepped out of the van and walked up to knock on the massive front door of the Moose house. Before they did, however, they heard voices in the backyard.

Biscuit led the way around the house, trying to be stealthy so they could overhear the conversation. Their bodies pressed against the side of the house, they were quiet, like a mouse trying to evade a cat. The words were becoming louder and clearer.

"Detectives came to see me today about Maple's mineral, Huck. They're bound to come here next to question you. What are you going to tell them?" Huck was taller than Liam, massive in size and as brown as melted fudge. His antlers were tall and wide as he shook his head from side to side.

"I don't know. The truth would be best, but I'll get into trouble for what I did."

Huckleberry glanced towards the house. Joe-Joe and Biscuit guessed he was looking toward the kitchen. They were crouched under one kitchen window, and heard the sounds of Mrs. Moose making dinner.

"I got to go," said Huckleberry. "Thanks for the warning, Liam. I appreciate it. I'll stop by later."

Liam nodded and ran towards the trees. Huckleberry slowly turned around and headed inside through their sliding back door.

Joe-Joe and Biscuit glanced at each other and smiled before working their way back to the front of the house. Once at the door again, Biscuit knocked loudly. After several minutes, the door opened wide. Standing in the doorway was Mama Moose. She was wearing a yellow dress and had a pretty bow in her hair.

"Can I help you?" she asked curtly, looking down at them.

"Yes, ma'am. I'm Biscuit Bill and this is my partner, Joe-Joe Nut. We're detectives on the case of a missing mineral. Is Huckleberry home?"

Mama Moose didn't appear happy as she glanced back inside of the house. "Did he do something wrong?"

"We don't know yet, ma'am. Maple Moo is missing a very expensive mineral. It disappeared sometime during or after Huckleberry and his friends visited her this morning. We're just trying to find out the facts, ma'am," said Biscuit.

Mama Moose was less than pleased. Her eyes narrowed to slits. She then bellowed loudly for Huckleberry, causing Joe-Joe and Biscuit to cringe from the sound. Huckleberry rushed to the door towards them.

"Yes, Mama?"

"HUCKLEBERRY MERRYWETHER MOOSE!"

"Huckleberry Merrywether Moose! Do you know anything about Maple Moo's missing mineral?" The question was blunt and straight forward. This female meant business.

Huckleberry looked shocked and shook his massive head, then he nodded briefly. Then there was a mixture of nods and head shakes. He didn't know how to answer.

Mama Moose took a deep cleansing breath. "You will stand here and talk to these detectives. You will tell them what you know about this missing mineral, and if you lie, you will not be able to play with Liam for a month. I told you he was a bad influence anyway, filling your head with all of this rock conference nonsense, and then your father with all of his sedimentary rocks he brings home to add to your collection. What a mess," spouted Mama Moose angrily as she walked off into the kitchen in a huff.

Biscuit and Joe-Joe felt bad for Huckleberry. If he had committed the crime, had taken Maple's mineral, he was toast. He had one tough mama. Joe-Joe was about to ask Huckleberry the same questions he had asked the others, but realized he didn't have too. This was going to be easy.

"So, Huck," he began. "You collect sedimentary rocks?"

Huckleberry nodded his massive antlered head.

"What are some kinds that you collect?"

Huckleberry held up a hoof for them to wait and disappeared into the huge house to gather his collection. When he returned Joe-Joe and Biscuit saw that he also kept his specimens

in plastic boxes the way Maple Moo did and each box was labeled.

"Do you know much about sedimentary rocks?" Huckleberry asked.

"We're familiar," stated Biscuit confidently, though Joe-Joe was shaking his head in the background.

"Well, sedimentary rocks are formed by the accumulation and hardening of sediments over time. I collect three different types, which is why my boxes are labeled." Huckleberry opened the first box. "These are clastic sedimentary rocks such as breccia, conglomerate, sandstone, and shale." Huckleberry let the detectives look briefly at the rocks before he closed the box, laying it on the floor beside him before reaching for and opening up the next one.

"This box contains chemical sedimentary rocks such as calcite, halite, gypsum, some limestones, and rock salt." Huckleberry let the detectives peruse these again before putting down the case. He then lifted and showed Joe-Joe and Biscuit the last one.

"This case contains organic sedimentary rocks, such as chert, coal, and some limestones, which form from the accumulation of plant and animal debris." Huckleberry closed that case and put it with the rest on the floor.

Joe-Joe and Biscuit wanted to know more about sedimentary rocks, but they could tell that Huckleberry wasn't in the mood to talk about them, especially when he suddenly raised two hoofs and covered his eyes. After several seconds, he lowered his hoofs,

and exhaled sharply. His features looked sad and stressed. For a moment Joe-Joe thought that Huckleberry was going to cry.

"Why did you take Maple's mineral?" prodded Joe-Joe gently. Huckleberry took another deep breath and let his shoulders sag.

"I can't take it anymore. Look, I *did* take Maple's mineral, but not for the reasons you might think. I wanted to show it to my sister. She's in a wheelchair and wouldn't have been able to see it otherwise. She broke one of her legs recently. I had good intentions."

Biscuit began to shake his head. "Why didn't you just ask Maple if you could borrow it?"

"I did. She said no," replied Huckleberry.

"Why didn't you ask Maple to come over and show it to your sister?" asked Joe-Joe.

Huckleberry opened his mouth, then closed it sharply. "I didn't think about that."

Joe-Joe glanced at Biscuit as they both shook their heads.

"Where's the mineral now?" asked Biscuit.

Now Huckleberry really looked stressed. "I don't know. I really, really don't! I showed it to my sister, and then Liam came over, and I was talking to him. I left the mineral in the hoofs of my sister. At the same time some of her friends came over to say hello. I don't really know who they were. I don't hang out with them much. After everyone left, I asked my sister where the mineral was. She said it was gone. My sister's upstairs, but I'd appreciate your not talking with her and getting her more upset. She feels really bad as it is. I

told her I'd find it, but after searching the house, I know it's not here. One of her friends must have taken it or something. I don't know. I can honestly say, that, at this moment, I don't know where it is. I've been searching for another mineral to replace it, but it costs way more than I can afford. I don't know what to do. I'm so sorry, detectives. This is all my fault and not my sister's. I'm so very sorry."

Joe-Joe raised his paw to cover his eyes. He had been so sure they had caught their thief, but just that quickly his hope disappeared like s'mores on a summer night. Now they were back to square one, had a whole new batch of suspects to interview, and the question that needed to be answered was further from their grasp. They knew who had taken Maple Moo's mineral, but now, who had it? When this case was over Joe-Joe was determined to talk to these children about keeping their hoofs, wings, paws, or whatever, off everyone else's stuff.

"You need to tell Maple what you did, Huckleberry. Tell her the truth. She might be mad, but maybe she'll understand. At least you'll feel better. We'll do our best to find the mineral," spoke Joe-Joe.

"Here's our business card, Huckleberry," added Biscuit. "If you or your sister can remember anything else, or if the mineral turns up, please give us a call right away."

"I will, detective," replied Huckleberry.

Joe-Joe and Biscuit got back into their van only to stare out the windows, not sure where to go next. They needed to talk to Huckleberry's sister, but they knew that wasn't going to happen, especially if Mama Moose had a say in it. Joe-Joe pulled out the picture

of the mineral and stared at it for several minutes. He leaned back in his seat, raised his right paw to his forehead and closed his eyes.

"Think, Joe-Joe, think. The answer is in front of you," whispered Joe-Joe encouragingly. As his mind raced, he began to daydream, falling into a soft sleep, his body relaxing as he allowed his mind to wander at will, his thoughts becoming more organized. He imagined that he and Biscuit were in a dark and dreary cave, and in front of them, sitting on an ornately carved stone pedestal, was Maple's mineral. To reach out and take it would be so easy. It glistened like stars in a midnight sky, attracting their attention, luring them. There had to be a catch somewhere. Something wasn't right. Joe-Joe and Biscuit stood beside the pedestal, analyzing it. There was a circle in the center of the pedestal, and the mineral was placed in the center of that circle. *A TRAP!* thought Joe-Joe as he glanced at his partner, who was wearing a russet-colored fedora, which matched his own—they definitely looked sharp.

Joe-Joe glanced behind Biscuit, where he noticed a deep gap in the wall. The opening was barred like a cage. Barely any light shined through to reveal what was inside. Joe-Joe had an inkling that, if he removed the mineral, the cage door would open, unleashing a horrific Greek beast that would assuredly eat them both for dinner. Joe-Joe began thinking like an adventurer. He was suddenly consumed with the identity of Indiana Jones.

"Biscuit!" Joe-Joe's tone was firm. "A leather pouch, please."

Biscuit automatically reached into his magic pocket and brought out a tan leather pouch and handed it to Joe-Joe. Joe-Joe

quickly dropped to his knees in the soft sand beneath his paws and began to fill the pouch. Once filled, he stood up, staring at the tempting mineral. Periodically, Joe-Joe would test the weight in his paw, let some sand out, then feel the weight again, letting even more sand out. When he felt the weight was just right, he raised his paw over the mineral. Before he grabbed the mineral to make the switch with the leather pouch, his eyes caught something move in the cave. It was a thick golden rope that swayed back and forth in a smooth and lyrical motion, then disappear into the shadows. No, it wasn't a rope. It was a tail!

"Joe-Joe!" called Biscuit. "Joe-Joe!"

Joe-Joe jerked awake. Biscuit wasn't talking to him in the dream but was pulling him back into reality. He was shaking his arm.

"Wake up! This is no time to daydream. We have a mystery to solve."

"I KNOW WHO HAS MAPLE'S MINERAL!"

Joe-Joe sat up straight in his seat and stared at Biscuit, his eyes wide and alert. Then it hit him like a ton of bricks. He knew who had the mineral. He wasn't exactly sure how it came to be in his possession, but he knew who had it.

"What is it?" asked Biscuit, concern filling his features.

"I know who has Maple's mineral," replied Joe-Joe confidently. "Can I see your mineral book again real quick?"

"Sure!" Biscuit was confused, not quite sure what Joe-Joe was up to as he handed him the book. Joe-Joe swiftly flipped through the pages to where the information for the mineral was located. He read the information, learning that the mineral had some special properties. Joe-Joe closed the book and glanced at Biscuit.

"We need to go to the high school for a minute and pick-up something. I have an idea."

Biscuit started the van and backed out of Huckleberry's driveway, then headed down the road. On the way, Joe-Joe told Biscuit his idea. They would soon see if it would work.

7
THE MISSING MINERAL

An hour later Joe-Joe and Biscuit were headed to the circus. After they had parked outside the main arena, they walked towards several small houses near the edge of the large red-and-white circus tent. The circus in Acorn Valley was permanent. Animals from near and far would come to see the shows. They did something new every few weeks, and their shows were always spectacular.

Biscuit and Joe-Joe weaved past the houses until they reached a larger two-story one with a lion's head on the door. Joe-Joe did not want to go inside, but knew he had too. Biscuit stepped up to the door and rapped loudly. There was no answer.

"They must be in the big tent practicing for the show tonight," presumed Joe-Joe.

So they turned around and headed for the main tent. When they stepped inside, it was like they were in another world. It was different then when they had been there that very morning. It was busier than a shark's pit at feeding time. Animals big and small were all practicing their performances. Each had an area in the tent they were focusing on. As the detectives looked further into the tent, they saw where the lions were busy at work. They were jumping onto large balls and making them spin while juggling. It was impressive. Artemus was talking with each group of animals as he watched their acts, critiquing them.

The lion cubs were practicing their acts as well. They pretended to be firefighters as they put out fires with large hoses. Their uniforms and helmets were all different colors. The cubs then leaped on top of one another to form a pyramid, the top cub flipping several times on top of the pyramid. Even the young animals were amazing to watch. They were all talented. Joe-Joe looked at the cubs. They jumped out of their pyramid then began to take off their firefighter coats and helmets, heading towards a room somewhere behind the curtain to put them away. When a lion cub in front of them took off his blue costume and helmet, Joe-Joe saw him. It was Arsalean. Biscuit walked up to him first.

"Hello, Artie!"

Arsaelan looked at Biscuit and then at Joe-Joe, his features calm and full of excitement. Gone was the scared cub from that morning.

"Thank you so much for helping me this morning, Detective Joe-Joe. I know I put you in a pretty good mess. My dad and I talked, and I know I have to stand up for myself. I had to stand up to Kojo, and, believe it or not, I did. I spoke with him and told him I forgave him for what he'd done. He and his brothers have been picking on

56

me for some time. My mistake was not telling anyone about it. I thought I could handle it on my own, but I couldn't. I feel so much better now that he and his brothers won't be bothering me anymore, and I do hope we can one day be friends. In fact, my dad thought of a great way for Kojo and his brothers to repay us for the broken equipment. They're going to work it off. They have to help every day in the circus tent. See, there they are now."

Joe-Joe and Biscuit looked where Arsalean was pointing. The brothers were in red-and-white pin-stripe uniforms picking up garbage between the rows of seats and cleaning up the area, making sure everything was ready for the night's show. Arsaelan was about to walk away, when Joe-Joe reached out and stopped him.

"We need to talk to you, Artie."

Arsalean glanced over at his father who was working with some animals in the main circle now, then followed Joe-Joe and Biscuit to a dark area in the back of the tent away from everyone's eyes and ears.

"What's going on?" Arsaelan asked curiously.

"Artie, were you over at Maple Moo's house this morning?" asked Joe-Joe.

"No. She and I aren't really all that close."

"Were you at Huckleberry Moose's house recently? This morning, to be precise, to see his sister?" continued Joe-Joe.

Arsaelan paused briefly, then nodded. "Yes, she's my friend. We didn't have school today, so I went over there before lunch with

a bunch of our friends to see her. With her broken leg she can't get out to play as much as she's used to, and I was concerned. Why are you asking me this?"

"Because," began Biscuit gently, "and I'm taking a risk here, but we believe you have something that doesn't belong to you."

Arsalean laid his costume on the ground, his features filled with curiosity. "What do you think I have?"

"This afternoon I saw you holding something Kojo and his brothers were chasing after you for. At first I thought it was your lunch money, but the more I thought about it, the more I realized that you could have been holding something else."

"Like what?"

For a moment Joe-Joe doubted himself. Could he be wrong? But then he took a deep breath, positive that he was right. "Like a rock!"

Arsalean slowly reached into his shirt pocket and pulled out a rock. "This rock?"

Joe-Joe and Biscuit nodded.

"I found this rock on their floor by the door as I was leaving. I thought that someone might have tracked it in from outside. It's just a rock. What's the big deal?"asked Arsalean.

Joe-Joe glanced at Biscuit and smiled. "See, that's what I thought at first, too. I figured that a rock was just a rock and that it held very little importance. But during our investigation, I've learned that rocks do have a value and are very important. There are many different rocks that make up our earth, and each tells a memorable

story. What you're looking at is not just a rock," said Joe-Joe, "but a very expensive mineral."

Joe-Joe reached out and took the mineral, holding it carefully in his paws as he studied it. "This mineral is known as a combination of benitoite and neptunite. It's very expensive and rare. It was taken

"THIS ROCK?"

this morning from Maple Moo's house by Huckleberry Moose so he could show his sister. She dropped it on the floor, and we believe it was probably kicked around by your friends. You found it."

"How do you know that it's Maple's mineral?" asked Arsalean.

Joe-Joe walked over to a nearby box and set the mineral on top. He then looked to Biscuit who removed a small square light from within his magic pocket. He handed it to Joe-Joe.

"Stand back away from the light and never look at it," warned Biscuit to Arsalean. Arsalean nodded and stepped further behind Joe-Joe as he flashed the light on the mineral. The blue mineral sparkled. When Joe-Joe pressed a button, the mineral changed color and glowed.

"I can tell that you know very little about rocks and minerals, Artie. I didn't know too much either, until today. So I'm going to give you a brief lesson. The blue benitoite crystals are surrounded by white natrolite and prismatic red-black neptunite crystals in this mineral. The benitoite fluoresces brightly under ultraviolet light. What I'm holding is an ultraviolet lamp. It is capable of emitting longwave and shortwave light. It can make things glow in the dark, that's what fluoresce means," said Joe-Joe.

"Longwave UV light is also known as 'black light.' When you and your friends go down to Beaver Lanes to go bowling, they turn on a black light to make your white shirts glow in the dark. Isn't that right?" asked Biscuit.

Arsalean grinned. "You're right. My shirts do glow in the dark when I bowl there. I never knew that was caused by using a black light. I just thought it was cool."

"THIS LAMP IS CERTAINLY NOT A TOY AND NEEDS
TO BE HANDLED WITH ADULT ANIMAL SUPERVISION"

"It is cool," added Joe-Joe. "Now, there's also a shortwave UV light. This light can be useful to many rock collectors in identifying minerals, but a shortwave light source can also cause blindness, which is why I asked you to stand behind me, Arsalean. This lamp is certainly not a toy and needs to be handled with adult supervision.

Some rocks can glow in the dark with both kinds of light and some rocks can only glow with one type of light or the other. Benitoite happens to glow with shortwave light."

Joe-Joe turned off the light and turned to Arsalean. "So, this light proves that this mineral is Maple Moo's missing mineral and you need to return it right away."

"I didn't mean to steal anything, honest I didn't," pleaded Arsaelan. "I thought it was just kind of a pretty rock someone accidentally kicked into the house."

"We know," answered Biscuit. "It's all right. But you still need to do the right thing and return it."

"I'll go right away. Will you stay for the show tonight? I'll be performing my new trick."

Joe-Joe and Biscuit glanced at each other and smiled. "We'd love to come," said Joe-Joe, "but first we will take you to Maple Moo's house to explain to her what happened. Otherwise I know you'll get distracted. It's very important that you do this right away to clear up any misunderstandings. And, we need to solve this case."

"O—kay!"

Joe-Joe and Biscuit talked briefly to Arsalean's parents then headed with him over to Maple Moo's house. Huckleberry Moose was already inside explaining to Maple what he had done when they arrived. Then Arsalean explained to Huckleberry and Maple what had happened. He then handed Maple Moo back her mineral. Her face lit up as bright as the sun as she grabbed her missing mineral

and held it tightly in her hoof. She then ran to her bedroom and placed it back into its protective box. All was forgiven. The case of the missing mineral was officially CLOSED!

The detectives left with Arsalean and returned to the circus, staying for the show as promised. Arsalean and his parents secured them a spot in the front row.

WHEN THE TRICK WAS FINISHED WITH ARSALEAN STANDING ON TOP OF THE LION PYRAMID, IT WAS JOE-JOE AND BISCUIT WHO CLAPPED THE LOUDEST.

When the show started later that evening, they were awed and amazed. It was the best show they had ever seen, and Arsalean's new trick was saved for last. When the trick was finished with Arsalean standing on top of the lion pyramid, it was Joe-Joe and Biscuit who clapped the loudest.

THE END

DID YOU KNOW?

Quartz is the second most abundant mineral in the Earth's continental crust, after feldspar. There are many different types of quartz, several of which are semi-precious gemstones. Quartz is most commonly used in making jewelry.

Gemstones are classified into different groups, species, and varieties. You can get several different colors from the same mineral. For example, ruby is the red variety of the species of mineral known as corundum, while any other color of corundum is considered a sapphire, not a ruby. The mineral species beryl has several varieties such as emerald (green), aquamarine (blue), bixbite (red), goshenite (colorless), heliodor (yellow), and morganite (pink). What is extremely interesting is that beryl is actually colorless in its pure mineral form. It takes impurities to turn it another color. For example, beryl becomes emerald when it has a chromium impurity. Beryl will become pink morganite when manganese is added, and if iron is added, beryl will become aquamarine.

There are many different types of volcanic eruptions. To check out some of these, look at the following website: http://library.think quest.org/C003603/english/volcanoes/typesoferuptions.shtml. This website has tons of information including activities and simulations of

various forces of nature, like landslides, forest fires, monsoons, tornadoes, and much more.

Sedimentary rocks are formed by the accumulation of sediments over time. There are three different types: clastic, chemical and organic. Clastic sedimentary rocks are formed from mechanical weathering debris. Mechanical weathering takes place when rocks are broken down without any change in their chemical nature. The rocks are merely torn apart by physical forces, then pressed together again.

Chemical sedimentary rocks form when dissolved materials precipitate from solution. This type of chemical weathering breaks down the bonds that hold rocks together, causing them to fall apart, forming smaller pieces. Water is the main contributor of chemical weathering. The most common types of chemical weathering are oxidation, hydrolysis, and carbonation.

Organic sedimentary rocks form from the accumulation of plant and animal debris. Basically, an organic sedimentary rock is made from fossils and can be found on land or under the sea. The Great Barrier Reef off the coast of Austrailia shows organic sedimentary rocks forming.

SOME TERMS TO IDENTIFY ROCKS AND MINERALS

Streak- is a way to reveal the color of a mineral when it is reduced to powder and rubbed across a plate or a piece of unglazed porcelain. The streak reveals the mineral's color. Sometimes it is the same color of the mineral, but not always.

Luster- is the way light is reflected off the surface of a mineral. Some of the non-technical terms used are:" metallic, glassy, greasy or dull. Technical terms used are adamantine, vitreous, resinous, pearly, silky, splendant, shining, glistening and glimmering.

Transparency- Minerals can be referred to in a few different ways. A mineral can be transparent, which means that an object can be seen clearly through the mineral. Semi-transparent, which means an object can be seen through the mineral but not clearly. Translucent, which means light passes through the mineral but an object cannot be seen. Then there is Opaque, which is when no light passes through at all.

Hardness- is measured by how hard a mineral is to scratch or to be scratched. It is measured by using the Moh Scale. The scale was named after a mineralogist named Moh. He developed a scale from

one to ten to rate hardness, one being the softest, which is talc, and ten being the hardest, which is a diamond. As we all know, a diamond cannot be scratched.

Tenacity- describes how easily a mineral can be cut. Some terms used are: sectile, brittle, malleable, and flexible.

Cleavage- is how minerals tend to break along definite planes when hit in the weakest part of their structure. The break is described as poor, fair, good or perfect.

Fracture- some minerals give a distinctive kind of break when hit with a hammer. A few terms to describe these breaks are: conchoidal, subconchoidal, even, uneven and earthy.

Density- is the specific gravity of a mineral. It is its weight compared to water. It is how heavy a mineral is.

EXPERIMENTS!
PARENTAL SUPERVISION IS REQUIRED.

IT'S GOING TO BE FUN, BUT FIRST WE NEED TO GET
SOME MATERIALS TOGETHER.   FOR INSTANCE, WE'LL NEED:

LIMESTONE   **OR**   CHALK

OR BOTH FOR THE MAIN PART OF OUR EXPERIMENT

CUPS   **OR**    BOWLS

TO HOUSE OUR EXPERIMENT

 WATER

LAST, BUT NOT LEAST:

ORANGE JUICE

LEMON

SODA

VINEGAR

WE'RE ALMOST READY,
BUT FIRST...

WE NEED TO MAKE A CHART TO GAUGE OUR REACTIONS.

HERE IS A SAMPLE I MADE UP, YOU MIGHT WANT TO MAKE IT DIFFERENTLY, BUT THE MAIN THING WE NEED TO DO IS STAY ORGANIZED!

Reaction Chart - Chalk/Limestone

Acid	Reaction Prediction	Actual Reaction	Prediction Correct?
Orange Juice	1	5	No
Cola	2	4	No
Lemon Juice	3	3	Yes
Vinegar	4	2	No
Water	5	1	No

Reaction Scale - 1 smallest reaction - 5 greatest reaction

NOW YOU CAN COMPARE THE DIFFERENCES BETWEEN OUR ACIDS! YOU CAN EVEN COMPARE IT TO ME, BUT I'M BETTING YOU ARE CLOSER THAN I AM!

NOW, ONTO THE EXPERIMENTS!

Experiments

Want to try a fun experiment? This one is called:

Bubbling Rocks

Background information: Certain rocks with carbonate compounds erode or dissolve when they come in contact with a liquid that is acidic. Carbon dioxide in the atmosphere can sometimes produce rain that is slightly acidic. This is called acid rain. Over time, acid rain can erode away rocks leaving sediment. This process can happen quickly if a much stronger acid is used, for example, vinegar. Vinegar is a much stronger acid than acid rain. Limestone is a perfect rock to use for this experiment, because it is made entirely of calcium carbonate. It will give us the greatest result.

Experiment 1:

Place a piece of limestone in a bowl and pour a little bit of vinegar on top of it. The reaction is amazing. The limestone will form bubbles be-

cause the vinegar reacts with the carbonate ions causing the limestone to dissolve. (It will not dissolve the limestone completely unless you keep pouring vinegar on it, so only use a little, don't get carried away.) When the reaction is complete, remove the limestone from the bowl and look at the sediment left behind. There should be a layer of small particles of calcium acetate, a chemical made when an acid and a carbonate react.

Experiment 2:

If limestone is not on hand, repeat this experiment by using chalk. Chalk is also made of calcium carbonate. This experiment is one of a comparison, or cause and effect. Make a chart and label it. By using lines below your chart make a prediction of what you think would happen once the chalk is placed into the vinegar and into the water based off what you know. Use inference. Then, place one piece of chalk in a cup of vinegar and one in a cup of water. (Make sure that each cup has the same amount of liquid with the exact same amount of chalk. Remove all variables). The chalk should immediately start reacting with the vinegar, causing it to bubble and foam. After about an hour, pour off the excess liquid and compare the chalk that was in the water to the chalk in the vinegar. Is there sediment in the bottom of the vinegar cup? Is there any sediment in the water cup? Were your predictions correct? What was the same? What was different? Did the color of the chalk matter? Could it be a variable?

You can try this experiment again and again with different strengths of acid, making a comparison. Try lemon juice, diluted lemon juice, coke, orange juice, or anything else you can think of that is acidic in nature. Make a chart of the different acids and rank them in order of greatest reaction to least reaction, or most acidic to least acidic liquids.

I hope you enjoy this experiment and learn lots from it!

The Rock Cycle

MAGMA

crystallization

melting

melting

Igneous Rock

heat & pressure

Metamorphic Rock

weathering, erosion

& deposition

weathering, erosion

& deposition

heat & pressure

Sediment

Sedimentary Rock

compaction & cementation